T0298278

GRAND EUROPEAN EXPRESS

THE FRENCH LIST

Shmuel T. Meyer

GRAND EUROPEAN EXPRESS

TRANSLATED BY
GILA WALKER

LONDON NEW YORK CALCUTTA

This volume is part of a boxed set
titled *And the War Is Over . . .*
Not to be sold separately.

Seagull Books, 2024

Originally published in French as *Les Grands Express Européens*
© 2021 Les Éditions Metropolis, Geneva

English translation © Gila Walker, 2024

First published in English translation by Seagull Books, 2024

ISBN 978 1 8030 9 340 6

British Library Cataloguing-in-Publication Data
A catalogue record for this book is available from the British Library

Typeset by Seagull Books, Calcutta, India
Printed and bound by Hyam Enterprises, Calcutta, India

Ich grenz noch ein Wort und an ein andres Land.

I still border on a word and on another land.

Ingeborg Bachmann

For Rebecca

CONTENTS

GRAND EUROPEAN EXPRESS

She married the first to come along, the first who took it into his head to promise to protect her.

He was an odd-looking fellow with buck teeth planted in ruddy gums and eyes sunk so deep in their orbits they looked like agates in a puddle. His prominent cheekbones were framed by the sharp edges of his sideburns that he let run beyond his jawline, so that they practically enveloped his earlobes. She had noted minutely that this face, the face of her husband, already had the precursory asperities of his skeleton.

As she knew little of body chemistry, she felt neither repulsion nor desire, none of those misplaced judgments that provoke either disgust or attraction.

They moved, on the night of their wedding, into a small gritstone house with a low wrought-iron gate, flaking and rusty, that separated from the street the small, narrow garden, lined with box hedges on the right and withered rose bushes on the left. The house was a narrow, two-story building topped with a pointed red-tile roof, festooned in spots with lichen.

The kitchen and small living room on the ground floor were separated by a stump of a hallway almost entirely taken up by a staircase with beechwood steps, seasoned like the bowl of a pipe, which led creaking upstairs to two bedrooms. Adjoining the house was a laundry room which doubled as a bathroom and beyond that, tucked between the hedge covered with mauve clematis and the blind wall of the kitchen, was the outhouse.

Her husband's mother, who'd died six months earlier, had left on the dark wall in the hallway a poster depicting *Maréchal Pétain* in the field surmounted by the slogan, "The earth does not lie," and throughout the house a rancid smell and the sour memory of a lily-of-the-valley cologne.

The bedroom they chose by mutual consent was not the mother's. The son, because of all the memories held within its four walls of faded wallpaper; she, because of the insistent exhalation of ill-washed senescence and the stench of death overpowering the room and everything in it.

The newlyweds' more cramped bedroom had a window whose two top panes were opaque. Even on the sunniest summer days, only a drab half-light prevailed that hopelessly soiled the ceiling and its fake plaster moldings. This window, which barely dominated the garden hedge, offered a view of a strip of land abandoned to weeds and a dandelion-spotted embankment of ballast that rose to the railroad tracks and the beveled facade of the Simler & Bros factory beyond with its yellow brick wall that closed the horizon.

Every evening, once dinner was over in silence, he would go to the garden to smoke a cigarette rolled in corn paper. From the kitchen she could see the red glow of embers in the dark and the glimmer that lit the groove of his upper lip and his huge nostrils. He would stay there, without moving, cigarette clenched between his lips, hands shoved into the pockets of his overalls, legs firmly planted on the ground. Then, he would crush the butt on top of the low wall that framed the gate. He would do so slowly, with his yellowed fingertips, before burying the tiny stub moist with his saliva in the slanted pocket across his chest.

Fall had slipped away before its time. The cold had seized the valley with the cruel abruptness of traitors and barbarians. Toward the end of November, the ground was frozen, hard and brittle as crushed glass. The wasteland, under its glaze of frost, vibrated, crackled, and moaned with each passing railcar, before erasing its streaks beneath a fog more transparent than crystal. A powdery cloud, in the wake of the last car, descended from the tracks and came crashing against the back of the hedge. The water in the outhouse and the laundry room had frozen. At night, unmoving clouds hung by the hostile, round moon.

The house, which seemed narrower still, smelled from oil and from the embers that glowed in the bed-warmer. She was pregnant and would fall asleep in the acrid heat of her husband's body, her hands lightly resting on the top of her belly over her starched flannelette nightgown. In the morning, her breath thawed the frost on the fold of the sheet.

There was the first railcar that brought the sleepy, tightly packed battalions of Simler & Bros laborers to the city at the crack of dawn. Stony, taciturn men who had left their consolidated land parcels for the forge and its monstrous, blazing maw. There was the seven o'clock Micheline with the secretaries, office employees, and Aux Dames de France saleswomen. Then came the lengthy 8:10 train, majestically pulled by the put-putting green diesel locomotive. It crossed the city without stopping, with the arrogance of convoys that know only the light of capitals.

From her window, she would watch for the three dark-blue railcars bearing ten gleaming words stamped in gold letters over the entire length: Compagnie Internationale des Wagons-Lits et des Grands Express Européens. These three cars were like the three sapphires of a necklace, the coming into view, beyond the windowpanes, of a mysterious world of inaccessible exoticism. She followed the red lantern of the last car until it disappeared in the cruel light of the waning nights. For just a few seconds, the yellow windows illuminated the desolate landscape, adorning it with a string of supernatural jewels. Standing there, holding her breath so as not to fog up the panes, her left hand on her belly, she felt shame at the thought of the perfumed and sleepy refinement that must be observing her from the train, pitying the ugliness of poverty or laughing at it.

It had snowed on New Year's Eve and the sun would later give the whole white surface a clean brightness. Like a beautiful, washed shirt, with ultramarine reflections. No more asperities, no more trash. Simler & Bros' sawtooth rooftop was capped by a zigzagging frieze and the two blast-furnace smokestacks by bowler hats. Her head was still heavy from the plum brandy they'd uncorked the night before to celebrate the New Year. He was lying in bed, his jersey yellowed under the armpits and along the neckline, his mouth open to reveal his long incisors, yellower still. He snored contentedly from his excesses. Consolation hidden in the folds of drunkenness.

Her steps, light as they were, left footprints in the snow as heavy as a boar. The line traced was straight and cautious in the mantel that covered the wasteland, the waves left by her long, starched flannelette nightgown could hardly be seen.

She stood immobile on the tracks when the long train drawn by the green diesel locomotive arrived, blowing sprays of snow over her nose.

Like some cheap railcar, like a common Micheline, the Compagnie Internationale des Wagons-Lits et des Grands Express Européens stopped for the very first time at the small provincial station.

It didn't snow again before the following week and one could see over a good twenty yards how certain souls, powerless to hope, modified, imperceptibly, the railway timetable.

BELLA TOLA

One hairpin bend after another. The firs come after the larches and the larches after the birches. Behind the Postbus, the valley collapses in the unsteady buzz of streetlamps. Sierre recedes, and with it, all that Arnold knows of human beings and their mechanical power. The narrow road rips the dark rocks from the parapet.

This ascent of Val d'Anniviers, slow, noisy, and smooth, is a poor substitute for an assault on the mountain. The driver honks at the elbow of the tunnel. The horn echoes against the damp walls, swept by the glare of the headlights. The bus enters this belly of life in music. It would be absurd to say that Arnold feels small since humankind believes it can subdue nature with all its artifices of rope, steel, and concrete. No, what he feels is foolish, puny, and in love. He wants to look beautiful on the arm of the mountain!

He tells himself that this unmoving mass is the most spirited proof of supreme motion. He also thinks, as trite as it might be, that what the uncanny ocean hides from humans, these monstrous rocks reveal, with just the right mix of dread and joy to enrapture his love-struck heart.

He's overcome with unspeakable gratitude for its crests, jagged, disorderly, and uneven, standing out against the orange-streaked, dark sky like the broken lines of an electrocardiogram run amok. He's experienced the fear of oceanic abysses, the hypnotic fascination of the desert. Now, like a lover, he recognizes the sovereign splendor of the Alps.

The bus driver, in his blue uniform, holds the door open. Then with an exaggerated limp of his right leg, he accompanies Arnold, brings him his bag and his heavy, cracked leather suitcase. By the vehicle's yellow front with its smiling steel grille, the foreign visitor feels the engine's vibrating and reassuring warmth. He hands the driver a silver coin and thanks him. Between the pieces of his luggage, ramrod straight in his creased beige cotton suit, Arnold slowly fills his lungs with fresh air, replete with smells of fir, burned wood, and grilled sausages.

Bella Tola's facade is radiant. On the terrace, golden-yellow umbrellas are still open to protect a dozen guests from the dawning stars and a milky moon tender as a boiled bean. Women read in the light of oil lamps and hatless men play cards in the gray smoke of fat cigars. The night pronounces its sentence. Arnold falls asleep in the over-starched sheets after having washed up in a sink of white faience with an odd-looking brass gooseneck faucet.

Daybreak is pink. Between Frilihorn and Weisshorn, Besso, Obergabelhorn, and Cervin vie for the sky like little devilish milk teeth. Arnold slips on the clodhoppers he picked up in a specialty shop in Zurich a few days before. Heavy hiking boots of thick brown leather with bright red laces. It's the first time since the war ended that he wears his tartan-wool knickerbockers. He's lost weight. The fabric bunches up at the waist to form two unsightly folds. He doesn't give a damn. He buckles the silver calf adjusters. His white shirt's tinged with blue from the washing powder.

It's still too early for breakfast. The waiters and the maître d' are busy in the dining room, setting the table with cups, plates, and cutlery in a synchronized ballet punctuated only by the tinkling of the silverware. Arnold nods discreetly in their direction. His wide-brimmed, gray felt titfer underscores his emaciated features, making him look like a young Argentinian gaucho.

Arnold Breslauer walks briskly. Not at the sportsmanlike pace of his youth, no doubt, yet notwithstanding his gangly starved look, hikers crossing his path will take him for what he is: an experienced trekker, maybe a seasoned skier. He walks with long strides, his steps firm on the rocks, in the thick meadow grass, over the moraine-covered surface. He isn't short of breath. He holds his head high opposite the sun that rises over Weisshorn, setting the white roughcast on fire and brightening the wood of the Saint-Luc chalets.

It takes Arnold less than two hours and a quarter to reach Tête Fayaz and the Weisshorn Hotel on its summit. It's already half past nine. On the terrace, noisy and joyful vacationers. Mr. Henry, the owner, leans against the huge fir tree that shades the facade, observing with a satisfied eye the animation of his establishment.

Arnold takes a seat on a wrought-iron chair with a faded blue cushion, scraping the gravel underneath as he moves it, and orders a full breakfast from the waitress: tartines, butter, jam, Bircher muesli, and café au lait. Mr. Henry hesitates, approaches the newcomer's table, warmly greets his guest. The young man eats slowly. With the tip of his nail, he scratches a flake of rust off the white surface of the table. He stretches out his long legs, shuts his eyes, recalls with a smile August 8, 1937, ten years before the day.

It had been a long run over the meadows, thicker than a well-tended golf green. Sweat beaded on Antje Nussbaum's broad, round forehead. She'd gathered her long, dark, curly mane of hair in a wide, silk ribbon. Stretched out on the ground, her cotton skirt looked like a brown flower around her hips. Arnold had taken her shoes off and was kissing her small pale feet. Antje abandoned in the grass the book she was planning to read on the Weisshorn terrace and combed her fingers through her companion's hair.

Side by side, they blinked as they contemplated the sky of a cloudless world.

Wars do what wars must in accordance with their job description. Antje Nussbaum vanished in the snow of a vast Silesian plain.

Is he seeking consolation? Arnold thinks that Antje wouldn't have stayed with him, war or no war. She never finished anything, not her cup of hot chocolate, or the cigarettes with the silver ring that she'd crush nervously in Bella Tola's crystal ashtrays, or the book *La Petite Mort d'Aristide* by Magdalena M. that she'd forgotten on the table of the Weisshorn Hotel on the sun-drenched summit of Tête Fayaz that August 8, 1937.

Arnold heads back down to Saint-Luc, passes some hikers. Recognizes a hotel guest who'd been reading in the light of an oil lamp the night before, a sprightly woman in her sixties, with a tanned face. There are many daisies, bell-flowers, gentians, and buttercups too—white laces with yellow hearts—growing in swarms around the rocks.

The church tolls twelve. A scent of heather burning and hot resin floats in the air. The village is still festooned from the August 1 celebrations. The Postbus idles as it waits for passengers heading back down the valley. The driver buffs with a chamois cloth the yellow front of his engine, gleaming in the midday sunshine.

Arnold feels foolish, he'd like to be beautiful on the arm of the mountain, to be worthy of it. How can he be worthy of the mountain and the eternity that the most unjust of gods seems to have granted him?

Midway through the day, on the shaded terrace of Bella Tola, Arnold lovingly contemplates the fabulous peaks that rip the skin from the sky.

51 SHOLEM ALEICHEM STREET

He wasn't as famous as Amadeo or Chaim or even Mane-Katz, of course. But he had known Paris in the twenties.

Fresh from Lemberg, Galicia, Hillel (Steinmetz) Zerubavel had been dumped on the front, buried alive under mounds of loam and silt, trepanned, left lying under the yellow and rough sheets in the field hospital, and caressed by the swift, slender hand of Mathilde, the battalion's redheaded nurse. He knew Paris before and after the great butchery, Montmartre, La Ruche in Montparnasse, La Coupole, La Rotonde, the clap, Tonkin and Lea's opium, Bercy's doctored wine that burned the stomach, purple and cloudy as oil.

He'd knocked back quite a few with Utrillo and Cendrars, had starved with Kisling, had covered Kiki and Mado, Juana, and Rachel in kisses. He'd known Paris without ever attaining the heights of its museums, its galleries, or its salons. Hillel wasn't bitter or even upset at the "vay

13

tings turn," as he'd say with the Galician accent that he flourished with an impish touch.

Hillel was a happy man who celebrated his fifty-fifth birthday on May 14, 1948, amid the jubilation of independence. Through his open window at 51 Sholem Aleichem Street, he heard the crowd shouting and singing on that holy Sabbath eve. The national exultation, vigorous and vaguely childish, greatly boosted the ardor of the buccal tribute he was paying to the burning and slightly swollen sex of the revisionist Yishuv director's wife.

Hillel managed to make ends meet by painting family portraits which were popular among the middle-class Germans who lived in his neighborhood, institutional murals of pioneering rural life in epic style, coffeehouse decorations, landscapes, and local flora. Two passions in his indolent life: women and his Monet-Goyon S3G 100cm3 with bright-red enamel rims and reservoir. As far as the women were concerned, Hillel Zerubavel drew from the national supply without moderation and without scruples, with (to his credit) total indifference to age, social status, religion, or race. As for his motorcycle, as far as I can recall, there were only three in Tel Aviv, his and two gray Triumph 500ccs acquired from the stock of the retreating British army, two hot rods driven by Palmach officers, hair blowing in the wind and shirts open.

With utmost seriousness, Hillel described himself as an expresso-cubo-impressio-humanist, which was strictly nonsense since he painted in accordance with the appearance of the client or the landscape and not in an acquired style influenced by a school or a mode. This absence of genre was not to the liking of many, and though it discouraged gallerists and technicians alike, one had to admit that there was no lack of talent and often even of genius in this great pictorial mishmash.

On weekdays he painted in the studio-cum-bedroom where he received his models. On Shabbat, easel and canvases strapped to his luggage rack, he sped bareheaded, his cracked leather jacket wide open, to the orange groves of Rehovot and Gedera, to materialize his obsession with citrus fruits.

Hillel was a happy man, but his high spirits, like his art, were not to everyone's taste. Even his friends, the poets and actors he'd meet up with every day on the terrace of Café Kasit, could barely abide the perpetual smile of satisfaction on his thick lips. But bliss is not eternal and no one's safe from the misfortunes of love, not even a happy, fifty-five-year-old little painter.

Surprises often walk straight through the front door, ignoring windows and chimneys. Sometimes they knock before changing your life definitively and, intrepidly, you open the door.

In winter, you help them off with their coat; in summer, you offer them something cool to drink. The latter is what

Hillel Zerubavel did the day after the celebrations, which was also the eve of the war. She had the pioneer look of the Palmach's female soldiers, khaki shorts hemmed at the knee, a military surplus shirt unbuttoned over her upper chest. He felt an immediate urge to run his hand through her thick brown hair. He could imagine the knots and tangles that weighed down that formidable mane of hair duller than hemp.

The painter was amazed to behold a face he'd painted dozens of times in pictures stacked against his studio wall. A face initially painted from life then little by little from memory. He recognized the curves, the angles, the texture of the skin, the pout, the fine lines by the corners of the eyes that smiled without the lips showing a sign of amusement or irony.

The young woman looked strikingly like Rachel, a model and friend of the painter when he was exercising his talents in Paris.

No need in so few lines to build suspense. The reader will have understood, as Hillel did, that the young lady with the bronzed complexion of Israel's soldiers was his daughter. The child born of his wild drunken lovemaking with Rachel Kagan, the muse of Montparnasse, who can be seen in the nude on countless paintings by Soutine, Modigliani, Kisling, and Hillel Steinmetz, whose name was not Zerubavel at the time.

The great tides of the war, the bloody and charred backwashes of the Shoah, had spewed its bevy of survivors onto the parched land of Palestine. Annette, for that was her name, had found her father.

The following week was the brightest in her young life. The Haganah had given her a special leave for this heart-warming reunion. And the two would not leave each other's side. They could be seen astride the painter's red Monet-Goyon on the ever-sandy road that led to Haifa, walking on the beach, and sitting arm in arm on the Kasit terrace.

Rachel, the mother, had died of typhus in a camp in Silesia. Annette had survived Beaune la Rolande, Drancy, and Auschwitz. In this scintillating month of May, the young woman celebrated her twenty-fifth birthday with her newfound father. Nathan Alterman and Amir Gilboa wrote poems for her. Hillel drew her portrait in red chalk. He did so with his eyes closed. They drank two bottles of 777 brandy. The party ended in the painter's studio at 51 Sholem Aleichem Street to the sound of Marie Dubas and Fréhel on old phonograph records. Annette danced with a teenage soldier named Yoram Kaniuk. Bodies swayed with happiness and intoxication. Hillel Zerubavel had reunited with his daughter.

During the fighting in Lydda, Annette's Sten sub-machine gun jammed, and she fell under the bullets of the Arab Legion. She now lies in Trumpeldor Cemetery.

Surprises walk in and out the door. There are those to whom you offer something cool to drink, then your heart, then the immense sorrow caused by the absence.

HAMMERSMITH ODEON

In those days, smog grimed everything. Walls, windows, leaves on trees, souls. Souls most of all. It begrimed you from Battersea, then blasted Clapham and Vauxhall, before spilling into the Thames and heading off to devour West End. Those who still wanted to believe in the existence of colors painted their doors red, blue, or yellow. The smog scoffed at geraniums and petunias; the whole city belonged to it. Stones and people alike.

The factory where Wendy works is a hundred meters from Clapham North station. But Wendy never takes the Underground. Wendy doesn't have a car and doesn't use public transit. She lives in Clapham and never ventures outside her restricted circle, no farther than Brixton to the south and Stockwell to the north.

The factory has one story only. Five windows surrounded by bricks on Landor Road and, in a courtyard trapped by three ugly cement wells and strewn with cans and weeds, a crimson wood door in the rear leading to Fenwick Place.

Opposite the factory, rotting timber props support an old, derelict factory. In the morning, Wendy passes by holding her nose to avoid the stench of piss and shit left by the neighborhood junkies and cats, a stench that brings back to her lips the slice of Sunblest toast with raspberry jelly that she gulped down too quickly standing at the edge of the sink.

In those days, smog grimed everything. Hair, empty milk bottles left on doorsteps, pages of the *Sun* covering shattered windowpanes, gutted mattresses in the empty lot on Willington Road that no one thought of destroying or burning.

Wendy's three children are brown-skinned, three nippers from three different neighborhood Black guys who had no desire to be fathers. Wendy didn't want to be a mother either, at least not so young, but that's just to tell you what kind of trouble a pretty girl from Clapham, in the Borough of Lambeth, can get into at an age when girls in maroon blazers in the West End are going to school, planning weekend parties, and dreaming about slow dancing to the latest hits by Leo Sayer and Kiki Dee.

Wendy is the factory White girl, something nobody, not even she, seems to have noticed. In the batik workshop, there are six girls from Brixton and two Jamaican forklift operators, die-hard supporters of the West Indies cricket team, tuned into matches non-stop, transistors glued to their ears. Wendy's friend is Allyson. She spat her first brat out of her ass, as she says, at the age of fifteen. She's done every job imaginable: waitress at a fish-and-chips, cashier at Woolworth's, restroom attendant at Charing Cross, street sweeper. The factory suits her just fine, fifty-six pounds a week works alright for her. She doesn't like the chemical smells, as she says, but it's okay. That's just to tell you that, in those days, the smog wasn't the only thing to muck everything up.

Wendy's last guy, Clay, Reggie's dad, is doing fifteen years at Chelmsford. A damn bastard, to quote Allyson. Spencer, the first one, died of an overdose not far from the Willington mattresses. As for Jimmy, her second, he vanished into thin air. Even his sister has no news of him. And so it is that Clifford, Stanley, and Reginald, respectively ten, seven, and five, the brown-skinned boys of Clapham North, live with their mother without any paternal authority apart from fat Allyson's who has taken it upon herself to shower them with thrashings when they piss people off, as she says.

*

I want you the right way,
I want you but I want you to want me too
Want you to want me, baby,
just like I want you

Wendy shimmies lasciviously in front of her TV, swaying her small buttocks in her nylon panties to the schmaltzy sounds of the latest Marvin Gaye hit. The window is up. The Clapham sky is bluer than the Caribbean sky in the poster that decorates Cindy's, the Afro hairdresser on Bedford Road, bluer than the sign at the Gulf gas station. A blue like Wendy has never seen in her life. It smells of vanilla and chocolate, she thinks.

Wendy is giddy with glee, since happiness, the steady kind, is not in her mental vocabulary. Mark is still asleep, naked in her bed. The sheet slipped off and she sees his sex cradled against the white skin of his thigh. Mark is young, Mark is handsome, and he invited her to a jazz concert at the Hammersmith Odeon in a neighborhood on the other side of the river where she's never been. Hard to imagine, isn't it? (Thirty years living in London and Wendy has never been to Hammersmith, and I'm not talking about the theater. No, Wendy knows nothing, absolutely nothing about what's happening on the other side of the river.) Wendy took out a map of the Underground. The Hammersmith seems so far away, two transfers, and just to listen to jazz, a band she never heard of.

She'd have rather seen Diana Ross, Marvin Gaye of course, Harold Melvin, or Gary Glitter, but Mark's taking her to a Weather Report concert, and she thinks that the weather is good and that the sky has never been bluer than on that Saturday morning and that if Mark likes Weather Report and he likes making love to her, then it can't be bad.

Mark's not the guy for her. That I can tell you right off. A student, the boss's nephew, a 1976 summer job at the factory. A middle-class guy from West End, with middle-class West End tastes and ambitions.

Wendy is pretty, it's true, not a cover girl, but a pretty redhead with lots of freckles, and big pale blue eyes that eat up half of her lovely Irish face. Something of a Dickensian version of the model Twiggy, which can be appealing. Mark is a bronco, a bag of hormones, without a care.

You'll tell me that it's a fairy tale, but who can believe in such nonsense two and a half years before Maggie's arrival at Downing Street?

After the Hammersmith Odeon, Wendy discovers the cottage in Belgrave Mews. White-washed brick, green lacquered door, bronze doorstop. Tipsy, she finishes off a bottle of white wine and smokes a joint. The bed linen is white cotton and Wendy realizes that Mark must hate her garish, synthetic sheets. She leaves her jeans and her flowery blouse on the eggshell silk upholstery of the George III armchair, ashamed of her cheap underwear and her supermarket perfume. When she awakes, Mark's there by her side with a cup of black coffee, a strong brew. The window is open. Wendy first sees only the wild blue of the sky, then the rose bushes that climb all the way up the wooden lattice to the window. Deeply she inhales the vapor of their multicolored flesh.

In those days, smog grimed everything, and that summer's sun abused the poor girls of Clapham North.

You'd like to know how the story ends, would you? I'll give you two endings, one for a malt and one for a pint of lager.

to be continued . . .

ENDING # 1   Summer came to an end and what a summer it was! Water was rationed. No more sprinkling the lawn or car washing. Dishwater served to flush the toilets. Cockney had Mediterranean accents, the Tube reeked of sweat and the Serpentine was but a shallow pool for foot baths. Wendy went back home, back to the factory where Mark no longer worked (but that, you already suspected), and back to her three kids, Clifford, Stanley, and Reginald, who hung out in the street. She sometimes dances in her underpants to seventies hits in front of the mirror. They changed the name of the Hammersmith Odeon to the Apollo.

ENDING # 2   Summer came to an end and what a summer it was! A summer of restaurants, walks in Oxford, weekends in the Lake District, Joan Armatrading, and Stanley Clark at the Hammersmith Odeon, a beautiful dress and heels from Harrods, lingerie from Liberty, a summer of white cotton.

"It was a wonderful summer, wasn't it, Wendy?"

CAFFÉ GRECO

If happiness writes poorly, then misery scribbles.

Thursday, September 9, 1943

Clara Bassano obeys, shuts the shutters of the apartment to prevent the sun from fading the drapes and the upholstery. But the sun resists between the thin slats, bathes the living room in an imaginary peace, a mythical quietness of distant, happy memories.

It's not the precocious morning heat that imposes silence on Via Cisterno. Nothing induces torpor as much as fear. Now is not yet the time for sorrow. The tears will flow later, prophesies Clara with silent lips. The jasmine wafts its fragrance to a terrorized people. The jasmine is useless.

Where did she hear that Marshall Badoglio had signed the armistice with the Allies? Had she turned on the radio?

Had the lamps behind the ivory Bakelite radio illuminated the wallpaper? Where had she heard that the king and Marshal Badoglio had fled Rome for Brindisi? Had she heard the Panzerspähwagen rumbling down the Lungotevere?

"We won't write anymore," she said with utmost seriousness to Hippogriffo, the ginger cat purring on the sun-streaked rug. He keeps his eyes shut, only a slight movement of his face in her direction indicates that he's listening. "I won't write anymore," she repeated for herself, acknowledging the audacity and understanding the monstrous change that would inevitably occur.

*

The municipal employee Martinelli miraculously recovers his strength when the sweeping of Via Condotti is done and the stairs of Trinità dei Monti are perfectly aligned with the shaded stretch of the street and the emerald pool of the Barcaccia. He joins his cousin Mario, head waiter at Caffé Greco, for a real thick coffee in a real thick white porcelain cup. He sees the Piazza di Spagna crew looking for a cool corner for their break, brooms slung over the shoulder like the rifles of an army of tramps.

The café echoes with its own silence. The red banquettes are deserted. Cloth in hand, the industrious waiters clean the clean tables, polish the already gleaming counter, move the glass bells and the pastries inside them, shine the sparkling percolators, dust the pictures frozen in gilt frames. Martinelli and Mario sip their thick coffee in silence, reminiscing about the first customers, the morning regulars, Dona Francesca and her incredible colorful jewelry, Madame Ambassador Bérard and the ugliness that she carries with her like a convict his ball and chain. They recall the noble Galeazzo Ciano and his court of admirers, pederasts, and preposterous fascists. They delight in the count's refined gestures, the heavy aquamarine signet ring on his index finger, the feigned slowness he imposed on his appetite, and his way of wolfing down two or three *sfogliatelle* like a famished Livornese beggar.

Mechanically, Mario wipes with his elbow an imaginary stain off his immaculate jacket, readjusts the starched sleeves of his shirt, combs his fingers through his neatly slicked hair.

The Antico Caffé Greco on Via Concotti is waiting for the Germans.

*

Clara Bassano slips on a basalt-gray pencil skirt and adjusts her white silk blouse. From the dressing-table drawer she chooses the five-string pearl necklace and earring set that Giovanna gave her seven years earlier in Portofino. She trembles, hurts her ear, gives up on the earrings. Hippogriffo rubs his warm head against her leg as she puts on her heels. She scratches his throat, gets up, turns off the last rays of the sun abandoned by the shutters.

Via Cisterno savors lazily and idly the final moments of shade before the zenith. Petals of jasmine float on the surface of a soapy puddle. Clara exaggeratedly inhales the mixed scents of soap, provolone, and cold cuts. Yellow wax rinds and sticks of ash hang from the ceiling of the Paolinelli grocery. The streets know nothing of the destiny of the men and women who live there and never retain the sound of the footsteps that carry them away.

Clara doesn't meet a living soul on the Garibaldi bridge. Fatebenefratelli Hospital sleeps in its cradle of pine and palm trees. The water running between the bridge's piers forms a small turquoise cascade, with eddies as viscous as the skin of an eel. Clara removes her heels on the tightly wedged cobblestones of Piazza Campo Marzio, imagines she hears cries, and recognizes the voice of Umberto Saba—

> ... *aprendi*
> *da chi ha moto sofferto, molto errato ...*

Via del Corso. Life marches in step with death. Clara doesn't look for an arcade to hide her fear. The sun is too bright for this army of leather and steel.

*

Martinelli, broom over his left shoulder, joins his coworkers in the shady corner of the Piazza di Spagna, bums a cigarette off one of them, uses his butt to light it. He squints, thinks of saying something about the incredible silence that reigns after the flight of two doves. He has neither the words nor the desire.

He knows the woman who's just walked into Caffé Greco after slipping on her gray heels. He doesn't know her name, but he knows plenty of things about her, things he doesn't tell his municipal coworkers.

Mario says, "good morning, Signorina Bassano," recalls that he called her Signorina Clara before, but doesn't correct himself. Behind the counter, they prepare the young woman's tea, lift the glass bell, and place a *cannuliccho* with slivers of candied apricots on a thinly gold-trimmed saucer.

Mario thinks that Signorina Clara is sad because her friend Giovanna left and nothing and no one can make her laugh anymore. She asks for a sheet of paper. He brings one to her. He has lots of time. No one else has come to Caffé Greco since the news came of the king's and Marshal Badoglio's departure for the south.

In a turn of phrase as cutting as a thorn, Clara Bassano notes, "If happiness writes poorly, then misery scribbles."

When she gets up to leave, Mario, head waiter at Caffé Greco, feels in his bones that he will never see her again and that tomorrow, tomorrow no doubt, he will be serving Rome's German masters.

Clara, the Roman poet, daughter of Giacomo and Rachele Bassano, died on March 24, 1944, from a bullet in the back of her head.

LA LOUISIANE

Paris, at long last! I said to myself.

End of the line!

The black and red G7 taxi rattles on jagged cobble-stones. The driver's tight-lipped. He's a White Russian old-timer. I imagine him a proud descendant of a fallen dynasty from Smolensk or Saint Petersburg, a veteran of the Kornilov brigade. All I can see of him is the fake fur of his parka, his threadbare shirt collar, and, in the rearview mirror, his blue eyes with creased lids scrutinizing me with curiosity. A silent curiosity that seems to say, "By the end of the ride, my friend, I'll know everything about you without having to say a word. Twenty years at the job have taught me more about the human soul than all the psychological treatises by Dr. Freud or novels by Fyodor Mikhailovich."

New Year's Day. The scant few hard-working Parisians hurry along, battling the wind with their umbrellas. Blasts of large whirling flakes spur them to sustain this infernal pace of industrious submission. Under the arcades on Rue de Rivoli, behind café windows, waiters in black uniforms and white aprons bustle around tables laden with crispy Viennoiseries and steaming coffee for breakfast. Amber streetlamps, gilt vaulting, the elegant curve of the arches.

On the left, the dark facade of the Louvre gives way to the shadows of the Tuileries. Nested in the bare chestnut trees, lights float from the right bank. Red traffic light. A woman trips, going down the steps to the Métro. She clutches the railing. Her umbrella, still open, bounces down the steps. A gallant man catches her by the elbow. She's wearing a red coat. Green light. Place de la Concorde, glistening, swept by a few headlights, seems bigger to me than it ever had in my memory. We cross the Seine, sepulchral, dramatic, dark as the Acheron.

The ride comes to an end at Hotel La Louisiane, Rue de Seine. The driver steps out to open the door and help me take my valise out of the trunk. On his dashboard, a dog-eared postcard and a gilt statuette of a sun-crowned virgin. I hand him a banknote with the image of Richelieu. He frowns; his workday started with me.

The snow thickens, covering his synthetic fur collar. He digs into the pocket of his shabby parka. My bill between his lips, he counts the coins in his frayed mitten. I tell him to give me change for twenty instead of a hundred. Two gold incisors light up his smile.

Because of the official holiday I stay closeted alone in my room. I finish reading *La Petite mort d'Aristide* on my bed.

Later that day, in the hotel's cramped sitting room, a dandy in his forties, wine-colored jacket, turquoise tie, and matching handbag, sips coffee from a teacup. He has puffy eyes and practically no chin at all. Sunk in a brown leather armchair, he crosses his legs with the somewhat pedantic dignity of an oriental prince. We exchange a polite hello. He has no desire to talk and neither do I. Fumes from an oil-fired stove climb the staircase, settling in on one landing after another.

I walked the streets looking for an open restaurant. Buci, Mazarine, Guénégaud, and Jacob. Nothing open. Too bad, no Café Procope today! At the corner of Rue Bonaparte and Rue des Beaux-Arts, a Jewish grocer from Salonica sells me bottarga, a feta tiropita, and a half bottle of Raki. At La Louisiane, I find the man the receptionist fondly calls Monsieur Albert sitting in the same position. He accepts my invitation, and we drink the half-bottle together. He talks of Cairo, and of Christmases in Egypt celebrated twice, one Orthodox and one Copt, and of laziness too. Of walks along the brown river in Zamalek, and of noisy mornings in Al Muski, fragrant afternoons in the Al-Azhar Park, turbulent nights in Tahrir Square, or lyrical ones on the steps of the Opera House, and of idleness too.

I had a dreamless night. I fell asleep to images projected on the screen of my mind. Latrun Monastery, the first houses in Abu Gosh, the ascent to Castel. The corpse of Dovele, the corpse of Ovadia. The goats under a sea buckthorn grazing without looking at us. Hill 315, the dry stone of Jerusalem. I'm thirsty. The water in the toothbrush tumbler has a metallic taste.

My room faces Rue de Seine. I throw open the window to drive out the smell of my night, my body, the mold covering the walls, the eiderdown, the gray woolen carpet. Leaning over the balustrade, I draw on my Gauloise, exaggerating my exhalation to pump up the vapor. A truck unloads its cargo of carcasses. Two delivery men in white toques and smocks hoist the flayed beef over their shoulders. Streaked with purple blood, the meat drips on the snow. A Nicolas wine deliverer honks with impatience. His load clinks when the three-wheel vehicle jolts back into gear. A neighbor listens to news on the radio in a funny short-wave language.

All is quiet at noon. The office workers have stayed in the warmth and comfort of their homes. The empty Métro takes me to the Saint-Lazare station. I'd forgotten the sounds of the Métro and its hot-steel smell. I count the Dubonnet ads in the tunnels. The mica shines on the steps of the stairways. The voluptuous gust from the ballast. The scent of distant memories.

The day never really broke. The city still waits for a light that, likely, will not come. I stop at a *bougnat*, Rue du Rocher, and order a grog. The owner serves it to me and turns back to wiping the thick glasses for wine. He lines them up on the zinc counter like a battalion of one-legged troops. An Arab worker does his best to warm himself over a coffee spiked with calvados. The sawdust under his boots greedily soaks up a small puddle.

The wind sweeps across platform A, lifting newspapers, refuse, and train schedules, swirling, captive, under the axles of the train. Yesterday, New Year's morning, at a small provincial station, I saw a woman's torn limbs and shreds of a nightgown.

My train to Houlgate is scheduled for 1:45 p.m. It stops at Évreux, Lisieux, Pont-l'Évêque, Trouville-Deauville, and Villers-sur-Mer. It arrives at 4:31 p.m. A little girl opposite me traces patterns on the fogged window. Through her finger drawings, the Levallois factories and the dormant worker gardens along the Seine. The Seine that the train crosses, follows, and leaves behind. The snow stopped falling after Évreux. The fields are white. A dark hole rips the sky. Diamond dust soars as the train passes. At the long stop at Pont-l'Évêque, I get out to stretch my legs and light a cigarette. The provincial station and the biting cold sharpen my memory. I recall the famous actress who fainted on the platform yesterday. I followed her with my eyes when the train arrived at Gare de Lyon station in

Paris. A chauffeur hoisted her many pieces of luggage into a black limousine. I sniff the crook of my sleeve. Ruefully I note that not a trace of her haunting perfume has lingered on my tweed jacket. All that clings to the thick fabric is the thick smell of Paris.

The feeling of loneliness is never quite as strong as when it drives out the other in us. It assails me as I walk the deserted streets of Houlgate. Daytime yields little to the night. A lightless day dissolves into the dark. I easily find the house facing the sea.

From where I stand, all I see are the tops of the beach huts and the vast dark expanse of wet sand. Then, behind the living-room window, I see him. He's sitting on a long sofa draped in a tartan plaid. He's drinking a yellow alcohol from a large cut-crystal glass. Bulging out of his tight dressing gown, he looks like a fatty sausage. The gash on his cheek from the train jolting to a stop is hidden under an oversized bandage. With self-indulgent nonchalance, he reads the newspaper set on the cushion.

The door to the winter garden offers little resistance. I stand there facing him. He displays no real surprise. My voice cracks at the mention of his name and I can barely whisper my sister Clara's. He gets it. I know he gets it. I point the gun at his broad chest. He looks at me at last with sheer terror. I step forward and shove the barrel into a mouth that mechanically gasps for air.

After Pont-l'Évêque, it's snowing. My compartment is empty.

The porter at La Louisiane welcomes me with a friendly smile. "Ah, Monsieur Bassano, Monsieur Albert has been looking for you all day. He's waiting for you on the mezzanine." He hands me a bottle of chilled raki and adds in a low voice, "This is meant to persuade you, I think."

Monsieur Albert seems delighted to see me. He doesn't ask me what I did with my day, pours me a big glass of alcohol. Before him, an assortment of golden oriental cakes.

We talk of Egypt where I've never been, of Italy where I no longer live, of Israel, and of indolence too. At one in the morning, we go up to Room 58 to finish the bottle. He asks me whether I have a profession. I reply that I completed architectural studies in Rome not long before and that the war, the wars, made it their business to change the very nature of my life.

"What do you do now?"

I talk to him of Clara, of revenge, and of a sudden laziness too.

THE FULL MOON
BEFORE APOLLO 11

"Not much for us to do this year, Herr Schreiber. It's growing like weeds."

Konrad Koenig waves, adjusts his soft Wehrmacht cap, and continues on his way pushing a heavy bicycle equipped with an outdated system of coaster brakes. Horst Schreiber replies politely to his neighbor's loud greeting, follows him for a moment with his eyes, wipes the drops of sweat beading on his forehead, and resumes his hoeing. He removes the weeds growing between the gooseberry bushes. The berries are beautiful and ripe. Their green-streaked yellow color is turning a pale ochre that augurs their juicy taste. The raspberry shrub bends under the weight of the dozens of vermillion heads, early harbingers of a great harvest. Nothing stirs in the crushing heat of July. It's nap time. Yet Horst Schreiber notes that there's a breath of wind since he can smell the awful but reassuring odor of manure wafting from the Schmidt pigsty, even though it's at the other end of the village.

Everything is admirably calm. The poplar tree at the end of the garden stands unstirring. Kaiser, the cat, abandons his ginger fur in the shade of the stoop. In the distance, the brown and black foothills of the Bavarian Alps stand out impeccably against an immaculate sky untainted by clouds. There is something happy about this still and silent landscape, muses Horst Schreiber, who slowly resumes his gardening. He's a meticulous man, just like his mother, Uncle Werner would have said. He gathers the weeds, a mix of grasses and brambles already wilted and dried by the sun. As there are not many, he uses a page of old yellowed newspaper that he'd prepared on the thick, cropped grass. He'll roll it into a ball, toss it into the woodshed, and use it to feed the first fire in the fall, or maybe for a barbecue with the neighbors a month from now, after the Assumption Mass. The thought of the barbecue reminds him that he has some shopping to do. There isn't much left in the fridge and Horst Schreiber, a young man of tradition, can't conceive of dinner without leberwurst and edelpilzkäse. The bread just wouldn't taste the same. He also has to buy beer.

It's too hot to take the Opel all the way to Kempten. Apparently, the new models, at least the fancier ones, are equipped with air-conditioning. Can you imagine how much a car like that must cost? But then again if Apollo 11 can land on the moon, Horst Schrieber tells himself, then why couldn't an Opel have air-conditioning?

In the shed, unexpectedly cool, Horst sets his hoe carefully against the recently plastered wall. He should take the deck chair out after dinner and sit under the arbor by the hedge that separates his garden from Herr Koenig's. He'd drink his beer and enjoy the coolness of the dying day and the smell of the cut grass. He removes his shoes on the stoop, careful not to wake Kaiser, and places them gently on the double wrought-iron bar used to scrape the rubber soles in winter when the garden is soggy. In the corridor, he slips into his felt-soled slippers. The oak parquet shines with polish. Horst Schreiber glides like a cross-country skier. The cat flap clacks. Kaiser joins him. His owner sighs as he skates to the kitchen. He pours a mixture of milk and cool water into a chipped blue earthenware bowl.

There's something happy, muses Horst Schreiber, about the perfection of a house, shutters closed, streaked with sunlight. The massive clock in the entryway, with its smooth mechanism, marks a quarter past two with a sepulchral bang.

The Bohemian crystal vase on the lace doily that protects the TV set sparkles in a sunbeam. Horst sinks heavily into the big brown velvet chair with waxed armrests. The cushions sag under the young man's weight. He doesn't look thirty-five. The face of an adolescent, round, a milky white complexion colored with freckles brought out by the sun and prolonged exertion, and a head of red hair. He removes his socks to absorb the coolness of the parquet, finds the best position, closes his eyes, and abandons himself to the silence. Kaiser jumps up on the seatback, sniffs his owner's hair, and lies down with a yawn.

Horst Schreiber sleeps mouth half open. His lips are pale, and his breath has the sweet smell of mint candy. The three strikes of the clock wake him. He stretches and the ginger cat does likewise. He savors the calm inside him. The sun has moved, shining now on the amber liquid in the bottle of schnapps sitting atop the folding Formica sideboard, surrounded by six small lustrous glasses. In the bottle, a yellow pear swollen with alcohol seems to be drowning.

Horst Schreiber finally resolves to lift his massive carcass. A childlike hunger assails him. He goes back to the kitchen, with Kaiser following him like a shadow, hindquarters swaying, tail up in the air. He cuts himself a thick slice of bread sprinkled with cumin seeds, opens the refrigerator, takes out the butter. Before spreading it on his bread, he puts a dollop of the yellow grease on his fingertip and holds it out for Kaiser to sniff. He likes the rough feel of the cat's tongue on his finger. He covers his snack with a generous helping of bitter orange jelly. The cat sits and watches his owner slowly chewing. The clock strikes half past.

Herr Koenig returns at around five, his Wehrmacht cap on the back of his head. He glances at his neighbor's closed shutters and, pushing his antiquated bike, he lets out a deep sigh. The sun, already, is dashing past the Iller and spawning multitudes of sparks that shimmer in its gentle ripples. A light, soft breeze sweeps the village and the reassuring stench of manure from the Schmidt's pigsty across streets, paths, fields, and gardens. A tractor whirs and a radio plays the latest Beatles hit "Get Back."

Horst Schreiber unfolds the *Allgäuer Zeitung* daily and reads the long article on the Apollo 11 mission. He makes a note somewhere in his mind to watch the July 20 evening news. Is it reasonable to imagine men walking on the moon? he asks himself. After all, it's a hell of a lot more complicated than installing air-conditioning in an Opel! He smiles at Kaiser who's wearing himself out licking his fur.

He's about to drop the idea of going to Kempten. He has enough beer at home for tonight, then he recalls that he has no more leberwurst or any of that succulent blue cheese that has been the mainstay of his meals as far back as he recalls.

Before heading to town, he goes upstairs to his bedroom to change. His old greenish-gray army fatigues are not suitable for the city. Maybe he'll have a beer on the terrace of the Silberflöte, a nice, cold frothy beer with a golden pretzel. He puts on a pair of light-gray flannel slacks and a sky-blue shirt with an overly pointed collar.

Walking past his father's bedroom, he hears the old man moaning in his sleep. He cracks the door open. Hauptsturmführer Aloïs Schreiber lies motionless in his high, carved-wood Bavarian bed. He's sweating and his lips are trembling. His hollow cheeks are smudged with gray stubble, scattered like a neglected lawn.

Horst Schreiber watches the feeble movement of the duvet that his father's chest can barely lift. The room reeks of bad breath and sour perspiration. The old man's head is tilted to one side; he must confusedly sense the corpulent presence of his only son. He shudders.

Horst leans with all his weight on the pillow. Disgusted by the sweat stains dotting the white pillowcase. A slight nervous kick of the foot at the bottom of the bed. His father's body moves no more.

He empties all the frames and medals decorating the fireplace mantel into a big red and gold plastic bag from the *Bayerische Zahler*. A clinking of shattered glass, knick-knacks, and scrap metal.

Horst Schreiber leaves the house, pets Kaiser's silky ginger hair, opens the rear left door of the champagne-colored Opel Kadett and tosses the bag on the seat.

As he drives to Kempten, with his windows rolled down, he thinks that tonight will be the night of the full moon and that he should observe it attentively, still virgin and pure, before human beings come to sully it.

SAINT-MAURICE STUDIOS

"You're absolutely right, Denise. Under the sway of intense emotions, you can lose your head and let animal appetites get the better of you. Let me tell you about something that happened to me about ten years ago that I've kept to myself all this time."

At this point, G. stopped. Her face colored as if an invisible director had slipped a filter in front of his lens. I sensed that she was torn between the pleasure of divulging everything and the desire to hold onto the secret, to keep the event warm in the depths of her memory or her womb. She proceeded nonetheless, but not before lowering her eyes and gracefully bringing her hand to her lips.

Here is the story she told me.

*

Without that tragic stop at the provincial station, I'd never have uttered a word to him. I no longer recall the name of the town where we stopped. It seemed so gloomy. It was snowing heavily, and I remarked to myself that the snow-flakes looked like soft white down. I was missing Venice and was apprehensive about returning to Paris. I hadn't slept a wink all night. I was waiting for eight o'clock to go to the dining car for breakfast and get out of the suffocating heat of my compartment. The conductor looked surprised to see me there and to hear that I didn't want to be served in my compartment. He readily obliged me, snapped his fingers at a waiter who then set a table for me. He was a bashful boy who smelled of the countryside. The cuffs of his white shirt were a bit too short, a bit too tight, exposing his thick gnarled hands. He blushed as he put the cutlery down in front of me. I was used to it, as you know. I was already famous and featured on the covers of motion-picture magazines. Most people found me pretty and I won't be hypocritical and deny that it was an opinion I shared. The waiter had a cowlick on top of his head that didn't give two hoots about the lavish amount of gel he'd applied to try to tame it.

He arrived a few minutes after me. I'd noticed him the night before in the same car. We were in the Lausanne train station. He was alone, awkward. He smiled to keep up a semblance of composure, fiddled with the food on his plate, without ever getting his fork to cover the distance between the plate and his mouth.

There was nothing special about him, if that's what you want to know. He wasn't Gérard Philipe or Clark Gable. More of the Marxist, intellectual type who'd somehow strayed into a luxury train. Beautiful eyes, yes that he had. Soft beautiful eyes, very black, but his hair was too long.

So there we were. I was sitting by the dark pane, waiting for my coffee and he was on his way to another table when the train braked with inconceivable force.

The night was lit by thousands of sparks shooting from the blocked wheels on the tracks. The stranger lurched forward to his knees on top of the waiter who was already sprawled on the floor. I slammed into the table. Dishes came crashing onto the seats. Some lights went out.

It was somewhat apocalyptic, now that I think of it.

The train continued on its way, nevertheless, to a small station whose name I can't recall. A provincial station partly covered with a glass roof. Despite the darkness, a trail of light revealed the long gloomy wall of a factory with a sawtooth rooftop. It was sinister, Denise! The passengers were half asleep. There was, I recall, a fat guy in a robe who'd slashed his cheek shaving. He had half his face covered in foam and a bleeding gash running down to the fatty tissue of his neck. There were women in nightgowns. Silk and see-through nighties. Yacking and chattering. It was terrible. The stranger stood up and helped the waiter to his feet. The maître d' tried to calm the travelers. He was a professional in full command of his nerves. He had a calm manner and a deep, reassuring voice that sedated us in English, Italian, French, and German.

After a few long minutes, I climbed down to the platform. The cold slapped me in the face. Bundled in a fur-lined coat, the station master was talking with agitation to the driver and a mechanic. I was walking along the platform when I noticed a strip of white fabric hanging from the footboard of the railcar, then blood, then what must have been a mangled arm. I collapsed in the snow, Denise, literally fainted. I only came to, believe it or not, back in my compartment. The guy I'd seen in the dining car was sitting on my bunk holding a vial of smelling salts under my nose. It was something straight out of a Labiche play, my dear!

He smelled of Yardley Lavender.

I saw nothing but his perfectly smooth cheeks, his long eyelashes, and his slender fingers. I shivered, he took my hands in his and I started to cry. He wiped my eyes with his handkerchief which smelled of his perfume and, I don't know why, Denise, I don't know why, but I sat up and pressed against him. I felt the buttons of his jacket against my chest, and I kissed him, Denise. A long feverish kiss that he returned. He took off my clothes and we made love. It was so hot, we were in a sweat. He sucked my breast like an infant, licked my underarms. I took him in my mouth.

He came in me like a hot spring. We lay there, pressed against each other in our sweat. He caressed my face with a bewildered smile.

In Paris, I caught sight of him from afar on the deserted esplanade in front of Gare de Lyon. He was hailing a taxi while the studio's driver loaded my luggage into the trunk of the limousine.

The next day, Denise, I was expected at the Saint-Maurice studios for the first day of shooting for *The Hunchback of Notre Dame*.

RED ROCKS OF COLORADO SPRINGS

It could have been any day. I didn't check the calendar that Mrs. Marthe, the head nurse, flips with great solemnity every morning as we enter the dining hall. Sternly she looks us up and down and only then does she moisten her finger, tear off the no-longer-needed page of the previous day, and crumple it between her fingers as if to let us know that we are now "one day closer to the inevitable!" It could have been any day. Except Sunday, the day when Mrs. Marthe is off, and Pastor Nicolet makes his weekly trip from Vallorbe to inflict his nasal service on us.

I was up painting early this morning. My hands are still smeared with black. Mrs. Marthe didn't say anything but even so . . .

Robert, the horse dealer from Orbe, drools into his bowl of warm milk. To the point that it's hard to tell the gobs of spittle on the surface from the thin skin of cooling milk. He sniffles. Wipes his big, pockmarked nose with his blotchy trembling hand. He's hung his cane on the back of the chair and his long frock of thick blue cloth, torn from the back cinch at the waist, floats on other side of the gnarled stick like two tattered banners from a lost war.

The rain is teeming down. This won't stop me from walking until it's time for lunch. It never does. I chose, to face this humid attack of autumn, the wide-brimmed felt hat that my cousin Charles-Édouard brought for me on his last visit. It's a hat from Ducommun of Neuchâtel that makes me look like a shifty, if not downright dishonest, Vaudois farmer.

As I expected, Mrs. Marthe confiscated my violin on the pretext that I could not decently play such a beautiful instrument with paint-soiled fingernails. She added that I was a degenerate and that my drawings would lead me inexorably to the Cery psychiatric hospital in Lausanne. She deliberately trod on two or three sheets of paper that were still on the floor, works I'd begun at dawn. Out of habit, I didn't protest. I was eager to taste the rain, feel the dying leaves, touch the soft, loamy soil. So to hell with the violin and Mrs. Marthe! I'll get it back next time my cousin or Mr. Ramuz comes to visit.

The rain falls stiff and straight like starched fabric. I pause to listen to its murmuring on the tiled roofs, its babbling in the garden, its tiny pattering on my umbrella, its mysterious humming in the forest.

Last night I dreamed of Madge. We were on our backs in a summer meadow, gazing at the sky. She was divining the shape of clouds and I was devising itineraries for the gaggles of geese and the scattered flight of passerines. It seemed to me that we were happy, that she loved me and that I loved her, that Colorado Springs revolved around our outstretched bodies and our hands entwined in the dry grass, inflamed with violent heat.

The soggy soil clung to my soles and the cuffs of my pants were caked with thick, dark mud. The still-tall grass had wet me nearly up to my knees. On the way back, I closed the umbrella to taste the rain as I'd planned. The brim of the felt hat my cousin gave me collapsed under the weight of the water. And so it was that I returned to the Ballaigues hospice all crusty and soaked. I was sorry there was no mirror for I couldn't see what the rain had transformed in me.

Robert the horse dealer, slumped on the bench that runs the length of the corridor wall, apparently lost control of his functions. A long golden trickle obediently follows the curves of the checkered floor from his slippers to the reception desk.

Does God never feel compassion? These smears of debasement, Miss Blandine, the nurse's aide, will wipe off the floor, while Robert will suffer Mrs. Marthe's debasing smears, as nasty as they are pointless.

Each day I note, with feigned indifference, the ravages that age inflicts on me. First it was my eyes. I'd rub them hard only to find a thin oily film on my fingertips without being able to remove the opaqueness of a white veil. Then it was my hands. I was unable to bend my fingers completely. The "electricity fairy" had amused herself by making the index and then the middle finger on my right hand tremble before immobilizing them like two angular fishhooks.

It all happened so quickly. After all, Pastor Nicolet's God has only nasal compassion for human beings.

I had to go to considerable lengths to counter Heaven's designs.

Now I lie on the floor to paint without brushes for I can no longer bend them to my will. There's something amazingly childlike about this new technique. I'm not painting what my intelligence knows or imagines about the world and people anymore. I'm painting what my body and my soul, together at last in this miserable heap of skin and bones, deciphers of the universe and its perverse agitation.

I know I'm being presumptuous in painting truth and yet I dream! I dream of Colorado Springs, its summer fields, its winter fields, its jagged red rocks that slash through the sky, sharp and bright as Madge's pupil. I paint the dark surface of humanity, the distorted face of my decapitated love, of my defeated heart.

On my return to my room I find the pages still there, scattered on the icy tile floor. Some bear traces of Mrs. Marthe's soles, her malevolent trampling. The rubber nodules have left flakes of coal amidst the writhing demons of my mind.

"Mr. Soutter," says Miss Blandine, the housekeeper from Lignerolle, who has the pointiest nose I've been given to see, "Mr. Soutter, your drawings are so sad and . . . (she stops to think as she tugs on her bottom lip with her nailless fingers) and . . . so mean." She seems sorry, doesn't want to hurt me. I tell her they're sad because God is mean. She crosses herself quickly and dares not meet my gaze.

"If I add blue, Miss Blandine, will it be less sad?"

She smiled before fleeing to the laundry room, dragging in her clogs. My fingers were blue when I got to the dining room.

"So it's not as sad, Mr. Soutter?" Miss Blandine whispered.

"Maybe, Miss Blandine, but God is just as mean."

Was the sign of the cross she made meant to protect her from the Devil or to drive Satan out of my body?

When I returned to my room, I found the violin on the duvet. Nestled in the down like a bird of prey waiting for me, ready to fly out of its hideout in the belly of the big red rock of Colorado Springs. I watched it for quite some time without moving. It frightened me. I heard its silent voice—an abandoned scherzo by Brahms demanding justice from me at last, Madge's sarcastic pizzicato.

Robert the horse dealer had a visitor. His son, judging by the resemblance. He sat facing the old man without uttering a word, without taking his eyes off him. Before leaving, he gently put his hand on his knee, then he delicately adjusted his greasy cap for him.

Tonight, by the light of the oil lamp, I think I finished my ink and gouache with the blue frock. I titled it *Good Father*. Miss Blandine's cross is there and, at the center, Robert, wearing the crown of the righteous. Madge is smiling to his right. The gate at the bottom is the one that closed on my mind and soul twenty-five years ago, when I lost the right to love the jagged red rocks of Colorado Springs.

MOONLIGHT IN VERMONT

The pattern of copper plates atop San Simeone Piccolo flickered in the gray sun. Myriads of droplets dissolved the Veronese green of the dome into its reflection in the troubled waters of the Grand Canal. The dusk gathered cold over the lagoon, early, too early for lovers of Venice's light who turn gloomy, melancholic, and feverish at night.

The esplanade of Santa Lucia station. Paths converge and diverge. Elegant women, municipal agents, newspaper hawkers with frayed mittens, porters bent over trolleys laden with trunks, newly arriving tourists, legitimate and illegitimate couples, street photographers bedecked with bellows and cases, scruffy kids hoping to catch a lira falling from a wallet, and then the arrival of a mahogany Riva amid a maelstrom of foam, and its passenger, standing in the stern, scarf fashionably abandoned to the wind, dark shades of feigned anonymity.

Because Venice is still Italy and Italy is always Italy, a young priest in a soutane and a biretta feasts his eyes on the film star's well-rounded rear end as a sailor lifts her onto the gangway, and because Italy is Italy, a nun with a cornette crosses herself several times perhaps to save the vicar's soul, to save the sinning star's soul too, and to cleanse her eyes from the sight of lewdness.

A well-born British housewife from Belgrave Mews arranges her daughter's pigtails while exhorting her three- or four-year-old Mark to stop playing in a puddle, shimmering iridescent in the cold sunlight.

Santa Lucia, though recently inaugurated, already looked like a ruin from an oil painting by Francesco Guardi, a flat and pale stage opened to the canal.

On platform 2, the tensions before departure. The relieved traveler embarking on an adventure. The anxious traveler forgoing the here and fearful of the there. The jaded traveler who knows the landscapes too well and has nothing to discover, neither people nor the sky. The actress from the mahogany boat signs autographs and excites the photographers. She's a Vestal come down amongst men to inflame the animal fire of their lust.

The compartments are fragrant with bergamot tea. Well-groomed waiters with old-world elegance help the porters hoist the luggage onto the train. The maître d' stops his tête-à-têtes with his small staff and begins issuing directions. A last magnesium flash on the platform. A fat man removes his wide-brim floppy hat to wipe the perspiration off his forehead. Too tight-fitting, the hat has festooned his skin in red along the rim of his hair wet with sweat. The train pulls out. The green diesel locomotive pulses, glittering in the rain. On its flanks, in place of the ocean resonances of its incandescent forebears on its flanks—the Baltic, the Adriatic, the Atlantic—its sole tattoo is an anonymous silvery BB 67035.

Rare are the passengers who stay in their compartments. The lounge car is a theater. To see and be seen. I'm here. You are too. The "us" takes shape around a shared privilege. A waiter—sleeves too short, fingers ruddy—serves flutes of champagne to the ladies and the effete. The men sit in whorls of cigar smoke swirling their scotch and amber cognac in soft waves and lending a distracted ear to the chatter as they wait for the arrival of the magnificent actress. What are they hoping for? They adjust their tie, throw out their chest, smooth their hair, wet their lips, pull in their stomach, remove their glasses, cross and uncross their legs, pull up their socks, straighten a crease in their jacket, look at their reflection in the panes or the bar mirror, ruffle the salmon pink pages of the *Financial Times*, or the ivory pages of the *Figaro*, the *Journal de Genève*, or *La Stampa*. She's not coming.

Holly branches with red berries on the white tablecloths and gold stars on the windowpanes remind some of the reason for their presence and others of human obstinacy in celebrating the passing of time. Crystal glasses clink and clatter, composing a childlike melody on the trays. The silverware and their sparkling reflections give the tables the appearance of a still life. In the tiny kitchen, the staff is busy preparing the dishes. The chef finishes hand lettering the festive menu in carefully crafted downstrokes and upstrokes. His mouth is watering as he does so, without knowing whether it's at the thought of the dishes or of the intoxicating lady to whom the menu is dedicated and with whom he is secretly and childishly in love.

BRESSE CHICKEN BALLOTINE WITH TRUFFLED FOIE GRAS

LOBSTER AND SCALLOPS

QUAIL STUFFED WITH ARMAGNAC GRAPES

PLATTER OF CHEESES FROM THE ALPS

ORANGE SOUFFLÉ CREPE FLAMBÉED WITH COINTREAU

CITRUS SORBET WITH STOLICHNAYA

~

CHAMPAGNE DOM PÉRIGNON

CHÂTEAU LAFFITTE 1947

CHÂTEAU YQUEM 1927

The night carries the passengers into the cold meanders of the Dolomites and the Alps. The fat man sitting at the bar orders a whiskey neat. His eyes are as glassy as a beached sheatfish.

In the corridor, an imbroglio of perfumes, cushioned voices, ruffled silks. The men for the most part strangle in the grip of their celluloid-stiffened wing collars. The women for the most part crack under their exceedingly white mask of rice powder.

At the center of the bar car, Red Garland smooths his small mustache before tapping the first notes of "Moonlight in Vermont" on the upright piano.

On his lips, the warm absence of a Mary Jane smoker.

The New Year's Eve dinner commences as they reach Lake Geneva and the sepulchral shadow of Chillon Castle. The train is blind, covered in a blanket of frozen snow. Mark and his sister are asleep on their mother's shimmering taffeta dress. At midnight, Red Garland breaks into a rubato rendition of "Auld Lang Syne." The Anglo-Saxons belt out the farewell song in drunken tremolos, while others kiss on the lips, and everyone regrets the absence of the stuck-up actress who had dinner served in her compartment.

No one pays attention to the chilled travelers who board the second- and first-class cars in Lausanne. The din of the banquet echoes under the station's glass roof. In the silent twilight of morning, the train nears Paris, travels through white fields, frigid villages nestled in the clutches of vineyards, wastelands, and residential districts riddled with chimneys.

Nobody in this blind vessel cushioned in frost pays attention to the painful destitution of the world along the edge of the railway and the yellowed windows watching the journey with no hope of travel.

RED ARMY FACTION

Horst Schreiber had hardened to carceral confinement by now. Stedelheim was a prison of the type they used to build in the nineteenth century and then modernize piecemeal in the twentieth. There was still a dining hall at its center, a huge, ice-cold, bleach-disinfected tiled hall supported by sixteen steel columns. Four rows of twenty-five tables and fifty benches, each seating ten.

Horst shared his cell with two fellow inmates. The older one, nicknamed Willy, was hunched like a beggar. The skin on his face clung to his bones, transparent. Thirty years he'd been there. For rape and murder. He'd survived the war without suffering much other than from the food rationing at the end. He was in his eighties. His fingers were twisted and yellow like the feet of a chicken.

He killed time playing never-ending games of Solitaire, as did Fernando, the wop, the other inmate in their cell, who jerked off four times a day and even five on the day of the weekly shower. The stud was a likeable, priapic pimp, a hustler who bought peace of mind by the shrewd distribution of cartons of HB cigarettes and porn magazines that who knows how he snuck into the slammer. It was rumored that his whores provided services apt to bend the prison staff to their will.

During a walk in the huge, fenced courtyard, Horst Schreiber had befriended Thorwald Wiesler, a lowlife from the local upper class. A liar, a thief. They shared what every young German of their generation had in common: Nazi parents. Thorwald was in awe of the older Horst for having smothered his sire with a pillow five years before. Triply in awe! Horst had killed. Horst had killed a Nazi. Horst had killed his father. The holy trinity of liberation.

From yard to chow hall, from chow hall to shower, the two had become inseparable. During the scorching summer of 1974, Thorwald Wiesler broached the political subject of escape with Horst. The two boys, who'd become lovers for the sake of physical hygiene, were not particularly inclined to convert to Marxism, but the thought of fresh air slowly worked its way into their minds tortured by the excruciating heat of the Bavarian summer.

At the time, it was not unusual, at a bend in the corridor, swapping a packet of cigarettes or an extra portion of leberwurst, to come across an apprentice guru of the armed struggle who claimed to have crossed paths with Andreas Baader or Jan-Carl Raspe at the Stammheim prison or Dieter Kunzelmann in Berlin and who, inspired by the righteous and noble cause, had joined the sparse ranks of the Red Army Faction, the Tupamaros, the Kommune, or the 2 June Movement.

No one, apart from Judge Jürgen Vogel, took an interest in their fate. Thorwald was released when his prison term ended and Horst, on the recommendation of this young liberal judge who was moved by the traumatic experience of the "children of" generation. Who knows why Thorwald didn't return to his life of petty crime in Munich, or Horst to tending his garden on the outskirts of Kempten. We lose their trail only to pick it up a few months later in an insalubrious, run-down squat on Ulmenstrasse in Frankfurt, which the municipality had boarded up with corrugated panels and wood planks and slated for a long-overdue demolition. Our heroes lived there with Kurdish families, South American prostitutes, hard-rock bands, runaways, and junkies of all colors.

Apparently Horst had swapped the silent use of a pillow for the noisier but evermore expedient Walther PPK 7.65. He and his companion held up Exxon and Chevron gas stations, and then hit soldiers' bars, all for the greater glory of the Viet Cong.

Their trail is lost again until November 1976 when Horst and Thorwald are seen in Beirut, in one of Dr.

Habash's PFLP training camps. There they learn their trade before traveling back home via Yemen and Bulgaria, and moving into a house in the suburb of Frankfurt.

Having gained weight, Horst resembles a bank clerk with an enlarged prostate. Thorwald has grown a mustache and sideburns. With his Hawaiian shirts and pleated pants, he looks like the pimp he was cut out to be.

Is it fitting at this point in the story to mention the arrival in Frankfurt of El Al flight TV720 from Tel Aviv, with an old Galician painter onboard, an elderly Jew, contorted with arthritis, who had once spent time with Utrillo, Soutine, Cendrars, Kiki de Montparnasse, and Kisling? Is it fitting to speak of the joy he felt at the belated tribute to his output by the Rothe Gallery, on Bethmannstrasse 13?

Hillel (Steinmetz) Zerubavel unfolds his finest suit of thick black velvet, smooths the old-fashioned collar with the palm of his hand, hangs it in the wardrobe, slips a gray knitted tie with red pinstripes around the hanger's wire hook. The starched white shirt is on the bed. From the window of his room at the Steigenberger hotel, he observes the snowflakes jostling in the wind and the heavy pewter plate of the sky.

"Land of Europe," he mused histrionically. "Ah Land of Europe, gorged with blood like a sanitary napkin, soaked with bile and rot, bristling with shards, bones, and nail clippings." There he stops, sensing that his anger cannot override the selfish happiness that invaded him when he took a deep breath of the snow-laden air and his body swelled with the memory of his youth on the same fertile, yielding, and green land of this continent.

Katerina, the gallerist, came to escort him to the opening. Night fell ever so gently, illuminated by street-lamps. They will walk the 200 yards from the hotel to the gallery, already shining with festive lights. On the window, the exhibition poster: "Hillel Zerubavel, Faces and Colors of Israel."

The consul and her husband are already there. A flute of champagne sparkles between their fingers. Friends the painter hadn't seen for ten, twenty years, maybe more, greet him with applause. The flashes of a photographer from the *Algemeine Zeitung* crackle with bursts of light. Hillel (Steinmetz) Zerubavel accepts all the overtures with grat-itude. Surprises himself talking about his work, explaining it, telling about his love of orchards, of women with wide hips.

Arnold Breslauer, a Swiss collector, purchases a painting depicting an orchard, a man sitting on a motorcycle and, stretched out on the ground, a girl with blue hair. The two men escape the stifling heat for a few moments. Outside, they lean against the window conversing in German. Hillel accepts the cigarette that Arnold offers him from a silver case. The Swiss collector lights up the painter's face with the flame of his lighter.

Copying them, Thorwald lights a cigarette. The head-lights of the microbus sweep awkwardly over the shining asphalt. Horst takes two Walther PPK 7.65s out of his shoulder bag, climbs out the side door of the VW van, heads slowly to the sidewalk on the opposite side of the street.

With both arms extended, he aims at the two Zionist Jews who are smoking in front of the gallery. The first bullets instinctively find their targets. The window shatters under the furious blast. The skulls of Hillel (Steinmetz) Zerubavel and Arnold Breslauer burst asunder in a chaos of glass.

THE LIGHT OF LOURMARIN

Magdalena had lowered the window of her compartment. Though not truly surprised, she was still thrown off by the violence of the cold. The brutal braking of the train had roused her from a sleepy stupor and sent the pile of books on her berth flying. The only volume that hadn't joined the others in their fall was *Helen's Exile* by her friend Camus.

On the platform of the small provincial station, a wind whipped particles of ice into hundreds of tiny hurricanes. A man was carrying the Italian actress she'd seen the day before in Venice, holding her in his arms like a sleeping child about to be put to bed. The stationmaster sought to lend a hand but didn't know where to put it.

When Magdalena shut her window again, it was immediately covered in a dense but delicate veil of snow. She tucked the folds of her negligee over her thighs.

She could not be an author who writes one book only, though the book is acclaimed by critics as a masterpiece, translated into all the languages of Europe and more recently into Japanese. *La Petite Mort d'Aristide* could not be the culmination, the end of her work. Magdalena trembled at the thought of not being able to create a universe comparable to the one she'd already brought to life. Would she succeed in retrieving in Paris the abandoned world that she'd been unable to recapture in Milan and in Rome? Would Paris be Prague?

> To Magdalena,
> *Helen's Exile*
> With friendship to slake thirst and dry tears,
> Albert

Everything in this essay by Camus that she'd finished by the time the train entered the Vallorbe station intimately commanded her to shake off the unfortunate clutch of the North and embrace the South and the blue of the Mediterranean. To renounce her belief in absolutes and embrace the uncertainty of beauty and tragedy. Everything told her to forgo inflexible judgements and contemplate at last the real nature of people and things.

At the Gare de Lyon in Paris, her publisher was nowhere to be found. The porter, elbow propped on his luggage-laden cart, offered her one of his unfiltered cigarettes of dark tobacco. She accepted it to pass the time. The esplanade was empty. The actress rode off in a long black limousine in a cloud of exhaust fumes. The man who'd carried her to her compartment was busy hailing a cruising cab. The cigarette pleasantly scraped the back of her throat.

The hotel room was draped in antique pink fabric. The narrow window overlooked Rue de Seine and its gray zinc roofs. The publisher had had an enormous bouquet delivered. Pointlessly it occupied the small light-mahogany desk, exuding an artificial scent of mock spring. Everything in the yellow uncertainty of the overhead light belied this sham season.

That afternoon Magdalena was introduced to an Egyptian novelist who lived year-round in Room 58. She found him clever and charming. He spoke of the manuscript he'd just submitted to his publisher a few days earlier and declared, upon his honor, his enjoyment of *La Petite Mort d'Aristide* which he'd wept reading. For her part, she wasn't familiar with his work and apologized for that. He'd laughed too hard not to have been somewhat irritated by her ignorance. Back in her room she discovered a kraft-paper envelope on her bed with the corrected manuscript inside and a dedication on the first page of onionskin paper:

For Magdalena
Before you,
Mendiants et orgueilleux,
Servant of the sun, jealous of the rays
that kiss your face,
Albert Cossery

As the feeble daylight totally vanished from the street, she felt the overpowering need to write. On her blond mahogany desk, now rid of its floral pretensions, she scribbled in Czech, in her neat, slanted handwriting, crowned with little hats and horns, "The man had no chin. His smile seemed to divide his face into two unequal parts." Then she drank the entire contents of a bottle of vodka dug out of the bottom of one of her valises, smoked a dozen cigarettes which she stubbed out in the toothbrush tumbler, and fell asleep wrapped in her astrakhan fur coat.

The next day, at a table in Café Procope, Albert told her in detail about his evening and the nearly sleepless night he'd spent with an Italian Jew. "A splendid subject for a novel, believe me, Magdalena. A character straight out of the neurotic mind of Dostoyevsky or Hamsun."

Then he walked her to her publisher, Rue Sébastien Bottin, and waited in the Café de l'Espérance on the corner of Rue de l'Université. After that, they strolled along the banks of the Seine, lingered at the green boxes of the rare bouquinistes open on that bitterly cold day, crossed the gray river at Pont des Arts, traversed the Cour Carrée, carpeted in a thin film of snow, passed the cart of a coal delivery man, heard the echo of his dappled Percheron's hooves clanking on the cobblestones of Rue de Rivoli, and saw the sparks flying from its iron shoes.

Albert worried when he saw Magdalena ordering her sixth vodka from the brasserie waiter and her eyes abruptly glazing over with the gloominess that women of the North mistake for melancholy.

"Didn't you tell me, Magdalena, that you arrived in Paris on the Orient Express from Venice? I heard there was a suicide . . . I'm telling you, that Italian Jew was a remarkable soul, a strange young man!"

Magdalena recalled the man on the station platform and his graceful load.

Albert continued his monologue to prolong the atmosphere of perfumed grace that envelops the storyteller as much as the listener.

"A calm young man, and yet scorched inside, with the determination of men oppressed by the weight of a mission. Such things can be seen in their eyes, in the way their pupils constrict, in the deep music of their slow voice, in the roughness of their hands. And then, he left. It seems to me that he'd accomplished his calling. I don't know what he did, but the man who came back last night was as surely free of his chains as he was moored to a nightmare that he'd just conjured. Magdalena, that man was an assassin."

*

June 1959

The sun is already high. Magdalena finds shelter in the shade, in the section of the terrace surmounted by a tiled roof supported by three Doric columns. The creeper running over their summits quivers gently in the mistral. The clouds are gone. Those from the day before have disappeared to celebrate the power and infallible azure of the sky. She keeps the pages on the table from flying off with the help of a yellow advertising ashtray. It's filled with butts and a cork. The emptied bottle is there, against the white wall. Magdalena squints as she watches the light striking the village and the cypress trees of Lourmarin. A wooden shutter on the top floor opens. She can't see her friend who says hello but she can hear the gaiety in his voice.

A few minutes later Camus comes outside to join her with a bowl of hot coffee. In his khaki shorts and a half-unbuttoned white shirt, he walks barefoot on the tile floor. He teases Magdalena about her pallor: "Enjoy the sun, it's yours for the taking." With a curious forefinger, he lifts the pages on the table and winks with his right eye. The smoke from his cigarette rises straight up—cheekbone, eye socket, forehead, hair. Intrigued, Magdalena's friend reads the last line: "I don't know what he did, but the man who came back last night was as surely free of his chains as he was moored to a nightmare that he'd just conjured."

Magdalena tells him she's just finished the book she started four years before in her room in Hotel La Louisiane. As he stubs out his cigarette and lights up another, one of those unfiltered cigarettes of dark tobacco that scrapes the throat, he asks, "And what will the title be?"

Magdalena fiddles with the yellow ashtray still smoking from the poorly extinguished butt.

"The Grand European Express."